# Word List

Here is a list of words that might make it easier to read this book. You'll find them in boldface the first time they appear in the story.

| | |
|---|---|
| Majesty | MA-juh-stee |
| marriage | MAIR-ij |
| peasant | PEZ-uhnt |
| oxen | OK-suhn |
| tailor | TAY-ler |
| muslin | MUZ-lin |
| practical | PRAK-ti-kuhl |
| curious | KYUR-ee-us |
| unhitched | un-HICHT |
| errand | AIR-und |
| impatience | im-PAY-shens |
| dazzling | DA-zuh-ling |
| sincerely | sin-SEAR-lee |
| familiar | fuh-MIL-yer |
| curtsied | KURT-seed |
| echoed | EK-ohd |
| knelt | nelt |
| musicians | myoo-ZI-shenz |
| cathedral | kuh-THEE-druhl |
| aisle | eyel |

# Barbie™

## The Peasant or the Princess

Grolier Books

Barbie and Stacie were tucking their youngest sister, Kelly, into bed for the night. Not yet sleepy, the toddler cried out, "Story! Kelly want story!"

"Yeah, tell us a story, Barbie," added Stacie.

"Okay, okay," Barbie laughed. "Settle down now, and I'll tell you my favorite fairy tale."

Stacie crawled under the covers with Kelly.

"It was a cold and rainy night long ago," Barbie began.

*****

Prince Kendrick splashed through puddles as he ran up the stone steps of the large, gray castle.

He hurried inside, took off his cape, and gave it a shake. A dozen servants rushed to greet him. One led him to a chair by the fire.

"Your **Majesty**," said a servant, "if we had known you were coming home tonight, we would have made a feast."

"Please, I'm fine," he told them all. "There's no need for any fuss." He looked up from his seat by the fire. He knew what they all were wondering.

"No," the prince said quietly. "The princess I went to visit wasn't the right one. She's not the one I want to marry."

The servants looked at one another with disappointment. They had hoped to be planning a royal wedding soon.

The whole kingdom knew that their beloved Prince Kendrick, or Prince Ken for short, had gone on a journey to find a princess bride. His father, the king, wanted to turn over the rule of the kingdom to his son. But it was tradition that before a prince became a king, he had to have a queen to help him. And so, at his father's request, Prince Ken had traveled far and wide, looking for a princess to marry.

The problem was *not* that there weren't any princesses. There were many lovely young princesses in the nearby kingdoms. But Prince Ken wanted more than someone with whom to rule the land. He wanted to be in love with his queen.

All of the servants except one left the room, knowing that Prince Ken wanted to be left alone.

"Do you think she's out there?" Prince Ken asked Alan, his most trusted servant. "I've met so many princesses. Maybe I'm being too picky."

Alan was very loyal to Prince Ken and hated to see him unhappy. "You'll meet the right woman soon," he told Prince Ken. "The problem now is telling King Frederick that the search continues."

Prince Ken sighed. He was not looking forward to seeing his father. The king had such high hopes for a royal **marriage,** and Prince Ken was about to disappoint him again.

"Don't let the others tell him I'm back yet," he said. "At least I'll have the night to think of some way of breaking the news to him."

But at that moment, a trumpet announced that the king was coming.

Prince Ken and Alan stood up as the music grew louder. Two knights entered the room and stood by the doorway. The trumpets stopped playing as a gray-haired, bearded man wearing a velvet robe hurried in. It was King Frederick. Alan moved to the side of the room and stood quietly.

"My son!" cried the king happily. "I didn't expect you back so soon!"

Prince Ken hugged his father. The king's eyes were full of hope. Prince Ken tried to smile.

"So," King Frederick asked, "did you like Princess Sarah?"

"Oh, yes," Prince Ken said quickly. "She

4

was beautiful and nice, just as you had said."

The king's smile got even bigger. "I knew it! I knew it!" he cried. "Wait until I tell the queen! When will you marry, my son?"

Prince Ken sighed. "I don't know, Father," he said. "You see, we are not in love."

"I don't understand," the king said. "Couldn't you grow to love each other?"

"Father, please," Prince Ken replied.

The king reached over and patted Prince Ken's shoulder. "Never mind," he said softly. "It's all right. More than anything, I want you to be happy. There are other princesses."

At the mention of other princesses, Prince Ken sighed again. "I know I'm expected to marry a woman of royal blood, but I've already met so many princesses, and they all seem the same to me."

"Not this one!" teased the king with a merry twinkle in his eye.

Prince Ken looked up and frowned. "What

do you mean, 'Not this one'?"

"Now, now, don't look at me like that," the king said. "It's just that there's one more princess you haven't met."

"Oh, Father!" Prince Ken groaned as he led the king to the door.

"She's lovely," the king added. "Trust me. She's the one for you. I'll even make a deal with you. If you and this princess don't fall in love with each other, you may marry whomever you wish."

"Really?" Prince Ken asked, his face lighting up. "Anyone I wish? Even someone without royal blood?"

The old king smiled at his son. "Even the poorest **peasant** girl," he replied. "I know you'll make the right choice, and she'll be a perfect queen no matter how rich or poor her family is."

"Thank you," Prince Ken said. "I am lucky to have such a wise and kindhearted father."

## Chapter Two

After the king had left the room, Prince Ken turned to his loyal servant.

"Alan!" Prince Ken exclaimed. "Did you hear?"

Alan stepped forward and walked toward Prince Ken. "Yes, Your Highness. This is wonderful news, indeed," he said.

"I'll meet this last princess to make my father happy. Let us prepare to go tomorrow," Prince Ken told him. "I want to be done with this business as soon as possible."

Alan raised his eyebrows. Prince Ken laughed.

"Oh, I know," the prince replied. "I'm sure the princess is lovely, really. But falling in love with someone should just happen. Planning for it doesn't seem right somehow. The woman for me will be smart and kind. She won't be afraid to speak her mind or take action when she needs to. And when I meet her, I'll know she's the one."

"I see," Alan said. "Of course, there's always a chance the king could be right, too."

Prince Ken had never thought of that. "Yes," he said slowly. "Tomorrow's princess might be the one. In any case, we must bring special gifts with us to honor her and her family."

"Leave everything to me, Your Highness," Alan declared. "I'll pack gold, jewels, and pearls and bring a fine white horse."

"Perfect," Prince Ken said. "We'll leave in the morning."

"As you wish," Alan replied. "Good night, Your Highness." Then he bowed once again and left Prince Ken alone.

Prince Ken crossed the room to look out the window. The rain had stopped, and the night was clear. Hundreds of stars sparkled in the sky.

"The stars are more beautiful than pearls," Prince Ken thought. He leaned against the cool stone wall. "And these rocks are much harder and stronger than gold. The simple things of the world are the ones that truly have the most value," he thought. "Would a princess feel this way, too? Hmm . . . that gives me an idea. There's only one way to find out."

The next morning, Prince Ken stood with folded arms, watching a wagon being loaded with rocks. He was dressed in simple clothes for traveling.

"A few more," he called to a servant. "My future wife will be very happy to receive them."

Alan ran up to Prince Ken, his eyes wide. "Your Highness, what is going on?" he gasped.

"Stand back, or your legs will be covered with dust!"

Prince Ken laughed but paid no attention. "Now hitch up the **oxen,**" he called out.

Two huge oxen snorted as a strong wooden bar was placed across their backs. Their shaggy coats were thick and brown, and their hooves were caked with mud.

"Have you ever seen finer animals?" Prince Ken asked Alan. "I think they are the perfect gift for a princess."

"I see them," Alan said. "I can smell them, too. But what of the gifts we spoke of yesterday? I have them all waiting in the royal stable."

"I've changed my mind," Prince Ken said with a smile.

Just then the royal **tailor** stumbled out of the castle door to the courtyard. In his arms were a dozen bolts of heavy fabric. He placed them on the seat of the wagon.

"Here you are, Your Highness," he grumbled.

"Wool, cotton, and **muslin** fabric for the future queen, as you ordered. But I beg you, Prince Ken. In my cupboards I have rolls of the rarest silk and yards of velvet. And I have enough smooth satin to dress the king's army."

"Please, Sir, take them instead," added Alan. "Even the court jester wears finer fabrics than these!"

"Have no fear," Prince Ken said, patting Alan's shoulder. "Any bride of mine will be far happier with these simple cloths."

Alan stared in shock at the wagon with the rocks, the big, sleepy oxen, and the pile of plain cloth. He gulped and turned to the prince.

"Are these really the gifts you are bringing to the princess, Your Highness?" he asked. He was afraid to hear the answer.

"Of course!" Prince Ken said with a smile.

Alan gasped. "Surely not, Your Highness!" he cried. "The princess will be most upset by a

joke like this!"

Prince Ken shrugged his shoulders. "It isn't a joke," he said. "And if the princess is to be my bride, she will see the value of such **practical** gifts. She will know how to use them."

"But, Sir," Alan begged, "everyone will laugh at you! These are things only a peasant could use, not a princess. What woman would want such things?"

Prince Ken was quiet for a moment. "The woman I'll marry, that's who," he said softly.

With that, he said good-bye to the **curious** servants and climbed onto his horse. "Coming?" he asked Alan.

"Of course, Your Highness," Alan replied. It was his job to look after the prince during the trip. He, too, climbed onto his horse, and they set off.

A dozen men on horses followed Prince Ken and Alan. At the back of the line was the wagon pulled by the oxen. People ran out of their homes to see the group pass through the kingdom. Alan was embarrassed and lowered his head. Soon the whole kingdom was whispering about what they had seen.

"The prince is going to meet another princess!" the people told one another. "And he's bringing her rocks, oxen, and the simplest of fabric!" They shook their heads in wonder.

Prince Ken, however, was pleased with his plan. Maybe this time *would* be different. He began to whistle happily.

"Your Highness!" cried Alan. "Please stop! It simply isn't right for the prince to whistle! What will people think?"

"They'll think, 'The prince has lost his mind, and now he's off to lose his heart as well!'" Prince Ken sang out.

## Chapter Three

As Prince Ken and his men traveled on,
they passed by villages and then fields. Soon they
came to a forest. They stopped beside a stream
to rest and the animals took a drink. Alan passed
around loaves of bread and a basket of cheese
and fruit.

"This is the life!" Prince Ken exclaimed,
scooping water from the stream into a goblet. He
drank it down. His bright blue eyes were merry
as he took in the sights and sounds of the forest.
Birds chirped to each other, and frogs croaked.
Otherwise, all was quiet. Even the horses seemed

to enjoy the calm of the woods.

*CRASH!* Suddenly the quiet was broken by the sound of wood cracking and water splashing. Prince Ken and his men jumped to their feet.

"What was that?" Alan asked.

"I don't know," Prince Ken said as he ran to his horse and jumped on. "But let's find out."

The prince's men followed his lead and mounted their own horses.

Just then a young woman wearing a simple peasant dress ran through the trees toward them. Her cheeks were pink from running, and her long, blond hair flew around her face.

"Please help us!" the woman cried when she saw Prince Ken and his men. "A carriage has fallen off a bridge into the stream. People are trapped inside!"

"Show us the way," the prince said to the woman. He held out his arm to her. "We'll get to the carriage faster if you ride with me."

The woman grabbed Prince Ken's arm, and he pulled her up onto his horse. Then the prince turned to one of his men and said, "Bring the oxen. We may need them."

The young woman led the men through the trees to the fallen carriage. It had tipped over on its side, and the only door was underwater. The horses pulling it had broken free of their harnesses and were grazing nearby as if nothing had happened.

"Is anyone hurt?" Prince Ken called.

The people inside answered. They were cold and wet, but not hurt. Luckily the stream wasn't very deep, and only a little water had gotten into the carriage.

"We'll get you out of there in no time," Prince Ken told them.

At Prince Ken's command, his men **unhitched** the oxen. Then they tied a thick rope to the oxen's harness. The prince tied the other end to the carriage.

"Someone has to stand in front of the oxen,"

Prince Ken said. "They have to be led up the bank. Where's Alan?"

Alan groaned. The thought of standing in front of those huge beasts with long, pointed horns made him dizzy. "Here, Sir," he said, trying to sound brave.

"No, let me," the young woman said quickly. Then she slid off Prince Ken's horse and stood in front of the animals in the stream. "Come," she commanded. "You can do it! Pull!"

The oxen pulled. The carriage creaked as it was dragged to the edge of the stream. Once the carriage was out of the water, Prince Ken and his men gathered on one side to lift it. They eased the carriage until it was upright. The people inside pushed open the door, thankful to get out at last.

"Now we just have to get the carriage up the bank," Prince Ken said. He ran to where the young woman was standing. Together they tugged the oxen's harness until the strong animals pulled the carriage back onto the road.

"How can we ever thank you?" the young woman asked Prince Ken. Her dress was torn and wet and her hands were muddy, but the prince thought he had never seen anyone more beautiful.

"It's my pleasure," he told her. "I only wish there was more I could do. What's your name?"

"Please call me Barbie," the young woman said with a bright smile. "And actually, since you asked, there is something else, if you don't mind. A storm has damaged the roof of our village school, and the stones are coming loose on the chimney," Barbie explained. "The people in our village can't fix it right now, because they're all too busy with their farms this time of year."

Now it was Prince Ken's turn to smile. "Lead the way, Barbie," he said. "By the way, my name is Ken."

"Very pleased to meet you," Barbie said.

Once the oxen were hitched back up, Barbie

and Prince Ken rode into the next town. Alan, the other men, and the oxen followed them.

Barbie brought them to a small stone building at the edge of a field. She pointed to the roof, where a large, heavy branch had caused the damage.

"It isn't safe for the children to go inside," Barbie explained. "The branch may fall through. It has already knocked part of the chimney off. Do you think the oxen can pull it off the roof?"

"The oxen are at your service," Prince Ken said. "But what about the chimney?"

Barbie smiled and motioned toward the rocks in the wagon. "Well," she said, "I was about to ask if you could part with a few of those rocks. I could use them to repair it."

"You will do nothing of the sort!" Prince Ken said. Then he laughed at Barbie's confused expression and added, "Because I will gladly repair the chimney myself."

"Sir!" Alan whispered. "You must not climb

up there. It's too dangerous!"

The prince pretended not to hear Alan. He carefully climbed up the rough stone wall until he reached the roof. "Toss me a rope," he called to Barbie.

Barbie tossed the rope to Prince Ken. "Be careful!" she called.

Two of Prince Ken's men joined him on the roof. They tied the rope to the branch and tossed the end down. Barbie unhitched the oxen again and tied the rope around the oxen's harness.

With a mighty tug, the oxen went to work once more. Prince Ken and his men guided the branch as the oxen pulled it free.

"Stand back!" Prince Ken cried as the branch slid off the roof.

It landed with a crash below.

"Chop that branch into firewood," Prince Ken told his men.

They quickly got to work splitting the large

branch into pieces. Prince Ken climbed down to join Barbie.

"That wood will come in handy this winter," Barbie said as she watched. "Thank you, Ken."

"My pleasure," said Ken with a twinkle in his eye.

Alan and the rest of the men watched in surprise as the prince began to make the repairs to the chimney himself. Alan could see that Prince Ken was trying to please the young peasant woman. Alan and the others joined the prince in his work while Barbie piled the chopped wood in a neat stack by the school's front door.

"Good as new," Prince Ken said as they put the last rock in place. "What do you think, Barbie?"

Barbie admired the careful job. "You really know what you're doing," she said. "I suppose you spend a lot of time doing this sort of thing."

"Why, yes, you could say that, I suppose," Prince Ken said.

Alan started to laugh, but a warning look from Prince Ken stopped him.

"Are you a builder?" Barbie asked.

"Well, not exactly," Prince Ken said slowly. He liked Barbie and was afraid she would act differently if she learned he was a prince.

Barbie looked at the cloth in the front of the wagon. "Then are you a tailor?" she asked.

Alan grinned as he watched Prince Ken blush. "No," the prince replied. "I don't know how to sew a stitch."

"Well, I do," Barbie said quickly. "This fabric is wonderful. It's warm and well made. May I buy it from you? I can use it to sew warm clothing for the schoolchildren this winter."

The prince didn't even think twice. "Take it, please," he said. "It's a gift for the children." Then he told his men to bring all of the fabric to the school.

Barbie smiled gratefully. "Thank you for all

your help and kindness," she said. "This village is very special to me. The king does all he can for the villagers, and they do all they can to help one another. We just built this school, and I help the children with their reading."

"You're a teacher?" Prince Ken asked.

Barbie looked away shyly. "I guess in a way I am," she replied. "But I still don't know what it is that *you* do."

Prince Ken also looked away as he answered. "I'm just a simple trader," he said.

But Barbie was not fooled. She had noticed his fine horse and the way the other men treated him with respect. She smiled playfully as she spoke. "You may be a trader," she said, "but you act like a prince."

Prince Ken took her hand in his and said, "And you are more a princess than any prince could dream of, my lady."

## Chapter Four

Alan watched with great interest as Prince Ken and Barbie sat down together under a tree. He had never seen the prince act this way toward anyone before.

"Shall I ready the horses for the rest of our journey?" one of the men asked Alan.

"Not yet," Alan said, never taking his eyes off the young couple.

"Who is that woman?" the man asked as he followed Alan's gaze.

"She might very well be our next queen!" Alan whispered.

The man stared at Barbie's rough, torn dress and loose hair. She did not look like royalty at all. He shrugged. It certainly had been a strange day!

Prince Ken was enchanted with the lovely young woman. At last he had found someone who knew the true value of practical things.

"Barbie, where do you live?" he asked. "I'll be passing through this village again when my **errand** is done. I'd like to see you again."

Barbie thought for a moment. "I would like that, Ken," she replied. "I'm so happy to have met you. But if you're looking for me, come to the school. I'm usually there with the children."

"It was my good fortune to have met you. I'm lucky to have been nearby when that carriage turned over," Prince Ken said. "But I'm sure a lot of men in this kingdom would have been happy to be at your service today."

"I do not wish for people to be at my service," Barbie told him. There was a bit of **impatience** in her voice. "I've had that my whole life!"

Prince Ken was puzzled. "What do you mean?"

Barbie stopped talking suddenly and bit her lip. She acted as if she were hiding something.

"You can tell me," Prince Ken said. "I can keep a secret."

Barbie laughed. "If only you knew!" she said softly. Then she quickly added, "What I mean is, I enjoy working hard, too."

Prince Ken nodded. "I can see that," he said. He still had the feeling she was keeping something from him.

"That's why I love village life," Barbie went on. "Here, people judge you by what you do, not by how you dress. How rich you may be or who your family is does not matter here."

"I think I know what you mean," Prince Ken said. "It's what's on the inside that counts, whether you're a peasant or a princess, a pauper or a prince."

Barbie smiled. "Exactly!" she said.

Their eyes met. Neither one spoke for a few moments.

"What about you?" Barbie asked the prince. "Isn't there a young woman somewhere wondering when you're going to return from your travels?"

Prince Ken almost told Barbie the truth about himself. But he held back, afraid of what she might think.

"There is someone," he told her.

Barbie's happy smile quickly disappeared.

"I must go and meet her," Prince Ken quickly explained. "I made a promise to my father. But I don't think she's the one for me."

At this, Barbie's smile returned. "How can you be so sure you won't fall in love once you meet her?" she asked.

Prince Ken took Barbie's hand in his and kissed it. "Not even the most **dazzling** princess could compare to the one who has stolen my heart," he told her.

## Chapter Five

The sky was beginning to get dark. Prince Ken didn't want to leave Barbie, but he knew he had to honor his father's wish.

"Sir," said Alan, "I'm sorry, but it's getting very late. We really have to go."

Prince Ken nodded. He turned to Barbie and said, "I must go now, but I would like to see you again."

"I'd like that," Barbie replied. "I must go, too. I also have a promise to keep."

"May I meet you here again tomorrow?" Prince Ken asked.

"Yes," Barbie replied. "I promise!" And with a quick wave, she ran across the field behind the school and was gone.

Prince Ken watched her go. As she left, his heart went with her.

Barbie had barely left his sight when Prince Ken made a decision. "We are not leaving," he told Alan.

Alan's eyes widened. "But, but, Sir!" he said. "What do you mean?"

"I want to see Barbie again," Prince Ken told him. "She said she will be back here tomorrow. But I don't know when. I cannot miss her when she arrives. Tell the men to set up camp here for the night."

Alan wanted to be in a warm, comfortable bed after his hard day. He wasn't used to working in the hot sun. Still, his duty was to the prince. So he went to tell the men they would be setting up camp for the night.

No one slept well that night. Prince Ken could only look up at the stars and wish the sun to rise on another day with Barbie. In their sleep, the men kept kicking each other and getting tangled in their cloaks. Alan was sure there were fleas in the straw under his blanket.

At last morning came.

"Good morning!" called a merry voice.

It was Barbie!

Prince Ken rushed over and took her hand. "I had to see you again," he told her.

Barbie blushed. "I was hoping you would still be here," she told him. Then she opened her basket and shared some warm blueberry bread with the men. "I wanted to thank you for your help yesterday."

While the others were eating, Ken and Barbie began to walk toward the nearby town. But Alan was following close behind them.

"Go away!" Prince Ken hissed to Alan.

"But, Sir," Alan protested. "What about your errand?"

Prince Ken grabbed Barbie's hand and together they ran. They ducked into an alley and giggled as they watched poor Alan race past looking for them.

Barbie gave Ken a tour of the town, calling out greetings to all she met. Prince Ken saw how the people of the town loved her and how much she cared for all of them. She proudly introduced Ken and explained to everyone how he had repaired the school.

"Oh, Mistress Barbie," one little girl said, "he's just like the handsome prince from the storybook you read to us!"

It seemed to Prince Ken and Barbie that the sun was setting even earlier than usual that day. The time had come for them to say good-bye once more. Sadly, Prince Ken watched her go. Then he returned to his camp.

Prince Ken was deep in thought as he bathed in the stream that evening. He thought Barbie was smart and kind. And, best of all, she seemed to care about him even though she didn't know he was royalty.

"The horses are ready, Sir," Alan said. "And two of the men will stay behind and lead the oxen. Shall we go?"

"Yes, Alan," Prince Ken answered. "Let's get this over with."

## Chapter Six

Prince Ken and his men quickly got on their horses and galloped through the woods. A full moon shone down on them, lighting their way to a huge stone castle.

As they crossed the drawbridge, Prince Ken tried to act eager to meet the princess. But all he could think about was Barbie.

Dozens of knights and servants met Prince Ken and his men in the courtyard.

"Welcome, Your Highness," a young servant said. "Right this way," he added as he led Prince Ken, Alan, and the others into the brightly lit castle.

"Forgive my delay," the prince said. "The trip was more difficult than I had expected. I hope the princess has not been waiting long."

They entered a huge room lit with hundreds of torches. Colorful stained-glass windows reflected their light. Lions and dragons were carved into the dark wooden furniture. Trumpets played as a servant called out Prince Ken's name.

At the end of the long room, the king and queen rose from their thrones to greet Prince Ken.

"Your Majesties," Prince Ken said as he and his men bowed deeply.

"We're happy to have you and your men as our guests," the queen said **sincerely.**

Prince Ken looked around the room. He wondered where the princess was.

The king seemed to read Prince Ken's mind. He cleared his throat several times before speaking.

"I suppose you're wondering why our daughter isn't here to meet you," he said. "Oh, dear, this is most embarrassing!"

The queen sighed as a servant led Prince Ken to a seat. "We feel terrible about having you come all this way for nothing!" she said.

"Nothing?" Prince Ken asked.

The queen took a deep breath. "The princess just told us that she has already met someone she wishes to marry!"

"We've been trying to talk sense into her," the king continued. "She just talks on and on about her true love!"

"Now, dear," the queen said to her husband, "you were young once yourself! Maybe Prince Kendrick can understand."

Prince Ken smiled. "I understand all too well," he told them. "Your daughter sounds very wise to me. Please give her my best wishes for a long, happy marriage."

Prince Ken bowed again before the king and queen, then rose and turned to leave. Suddenly

he heard a **familiar** voice.

"Prince Kendrick?"

There on the stone steps stood Barbie. But she no longer wore the clothes of a peasant woman. She wore a shimmering pink dress with a long train. On her head she wore a high, pointed cap with a veil. Her blond hair was carefully twisted into a long braid that fell over her shoulder.

Prince Ken was so surprised that he couldn't speak.

## Chapter Seven

"Well, I'm glad you've decided to join us, my dear!" cried the king joyfully. Then he rushed over to his daughter and led her to where Prince Ken stood.

Once again Barbie and Prince Ken faced each other.

The queen smiled. "Prince Kendrick," she said, "may it please you to meet our daughter, Princess Barbie."

Princess Barbie wore a playful grin as she **curtsied** before the handsome prince. The king and queen watched the young pair closely. They hoped their daughter would forget about the young man from the village.

"Princess?" Prince Ken teased.

"Please call me Barbie," she begged. "Is it all right if I call you Ken, Your Highness?"

Prince Ken nodded. He couldn't take his eyes off her. "Haven't we met before?" he joked.

"Perhaps in the village?" the king asked. "She was there just today, weren't you, my dear?"

"A princess in the village?" Prince Ken said, pretending to be surprised.

"I'm afraid our daughter sometimes gets tired of life in the castle," the queen explained. Then, with love in her voice, she continued, "You see, the princess often likes to dress as a villager and go out to help the people in the kingdom. And not one of them has ever guessed that she is really a princess!"

"Clever girl, wouldn't you say?" the king asked, winking at Prince Ken.

"Very clever," Prince Ken agreed. "But I think anyone meeting her would know that she is no ordinary young woman."

"And you are no ordinary young man," the queen said. "Don't you agree, Princess Barbie?"

"Indeed I do!" Barbie answered. She was unable to hold back any longer. She began to giggle, then laughed out loud. Her parents looked at each other in alarm.

Prince Ken began to laugh as well. Alan and the rest of the prince's men tried not to laugh. But, finally, they couldn't control their own joy. Their laughter spread throughout the huge room and **echoed** all over the castle. Soon everyone was laughing but the king and queen.

"Will someone please tell me what is so funny?" the king roared.

At last the prince and princess stopped laughing and took deep breaths. Princess Barbie smiled at her confused parents.

"Father, Mother, this is the young man I met in the village," she told them. Prince Ken bowed to the king and queen again.

It took a moment for the king and queen to understand what Princess Barbie had just said. Suddenly their faces lit up with joy.

The prince and princess looked into each other's eyes, not needing to say what each already knew. They were deeply in love with each other.

Prince Ken **knelt** on one knee. The room suddenly got very quiet as everyone leaned forward to see what would happen next.

Taking the princess's hand in his, Prince Ken cleared his throat and spoke.

"Princess Barbie," he said, "it would be my lifelong honor and joy to have you for my wife and queen. Will you marry me?"

Princess Barbie smiled happily as she replied, "I will, Prince Ken!"

The words had barely left Barbie's lips when

everyone in the room cheered. The king and queen beamed at the young couple and wiped tears from their eyes. The king turned to the **musicians** seated near his throne and waved his hand. The great hall was suddenly filled with music.

Prince Ken rose and took Princess Barbie in his arms. "I love you, Barbie," he said to her.

"I love you, too," Princess Barbie told him.

And they sealed their love with a kiss.

## Chapter Eight

Prince Ken and Princess Barbie wanted to get married as soon as possible. So the next morning, Alan sent a messenger to bring the good news back to King Frederick and his wife. When Prince Ken's father heard the news, he smiled and gave a sigh of relief. The queen was so happy, she cried. They made plans right away to leave for the wedding.

The news about the happy couple quickly spread throughout the kingdom. Their romantic story spread even faster in Barbie's kingdom.

The villagers were amazed to learn that the teacher they had grown to love was actually a princess! Much to their delight, they were all invited to the royal wedding. Everyday cares were put aside as everyone talked about the big day.

Inside the castle, the excitement was even greater. The royal musicians practiced from morning until night. The royal cooks prepared for the huge wedding feast. The royal tailor sewed beautiful wedding outfits, one after the other. Everyone was thrilled to be part of this happy occasion.

Princess Barbie's younger sisters, the princesses Skipper, Stacie, and little Kelly, were very excited, too. Princess Barbie had asked Skipper to be her maid of honor, Stacie to be her bridesmaid, and Kelly to be her flower girl.

At last the morning of the wedding arrived, sunny and clear. One hundred knights set out on white horses to parade around the castle. The knights carried flags and banners of purple and gold in honor of Barbie and Ken's royal families.

Barbie put on her wedding gown and looked at herself in the mirror. "This is a dream come true," she said with a sigh.

The queen beamed at her daughter. "It's perfect," she told Barbie. "Oh! I almost forgot!" The queen reached into a velvet bag she had brought with her. Then she gently placed a pair of sparkling glass slippers in Princess Barbie's hands.

"I wore them on my wedding day," she said softly. "Would you like to wear them today?"

"Oh, mother!" Princess Barbie cried, throwing her arms around the queen's neck. "They're beautiful!" She tried the slippers on, and they fit just right.

Inside the **cathedral,** Prince Ken stood straight and proud. In just a short time, he and Barbie would be married!

Music played softly as the bridal party slowly began its walk down the **aisle.** Everyone in the crowd smiled as Princess Kelly carefully dropped rose petals from a basket.

Then a hush came over the room. The bride had arrived.

Princess Barbie smiled as she walked down the aisle, her father at her side. She wore a beautiful white gown trimmed with threads of gold. Tiny white rosebuds were tied with golden ribbons across her full skirt. Her blond hair was braided and pulled back, and she wore a jeweled cap with a long white veil trailing from it. With each step she took, her glass slippers flashed in the light.

At last, Princess Barbie stopped beside Prince Ken. The music played on as the happy young couple promised to love each other forever.

"I will love you and honor you all the days of my life," they told each other. And they added a special vow. They promised to work together to improve their kingdoms.

As they sealed their vows with a kiss, a

hundred white doves were set free above the cathedral. Wedding bells rang throughout the land, reminding everyone that this was just the beginning.

*****

Barbie stopped speaking and looked down at the bed. Her two sisters were both fast asleep. Barbie covered them with a warm quilt and kissed them each on the forehead. Then, with a yawn, she went off to continue the story in her own sweet dreams.